Count the days to Christmas

Mary and baby Jesus

December 25: Christmas Day

At Christmas time

We shop for treats and gifts

We decorate the tree

We sing carols

We go to bed excited

find a sticker   find a sticker

find a sticker

We open our presents

What's inside?

Can you guess from the shape?
Can you find the sticker to match?

Christmas counting

5

4

3

2

1

Which way to Bethlehem?

Can you show the
shepherds the way?

Can you show the
wise men the way?

Pairs

Can you match each stocking to its pair?

Can you find a sticker to
match the one that is left?

Spot the difference

It's nativity play time.
Here are three wise men.

Can you spot the difference
between these pictures?

Can you find seven things different?

The noisy stable

Here is the place where Jesus was born. The ox and the ass are here, but where are the other animals?

Count the days
to Christmas
page 1

At Christmas time
page 2

What's inside?
page 3

Pairs
page 6

The noisy stable
pages 8-9

Christmas
gingerbread
pages 10-11

Christmas poem
pages 14-15

Christmas Journey pages 12-13

Decorate
this tree
pages 16

Put the right sticker on the animal shape.
Say the sound of the animal!

Christmas gingerbread

1. Ask a grown up to help with the cooking. Wash your hands.

2. Mix together in a bowl:
300g plain flour
1 teaspoon baking soda
1 teaspoon cinnamon
1 teaspoon ginger

Ask a grown up to melt together:
125g butter
100g brown sugar
2 tablespoons black treacle

3. Pour the melted stuff into the bowl.

4. Stir to make a lump. Chill.

5. Roll out the lump on a piece of baking paper. Cut into shapes. Put baking paper on an oven tray. Put the gingerbread shapes on top. Bake for about 10 minutes at 170°C. Leave to cool.

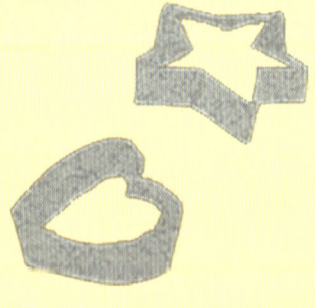

Decorate these gingerbread shapes using stickers
while you let your real gingerbread cool.

Then decorate the real gingerbread with icing and tiny sweets.

Christmas Journey

Choose a character sticker to play the race. Stick it on plain card and cut it out. Make number tiles on plain card with the dotted stickers. Place the tiles face down and jumble them up before choosing one to give the score for each go.

19

20
Lose crown. Go back 4 to find it.

21

22
CHALLENGE
Sing a carol or miss a go.

23

26
Socks have holes. Go back 1.

25

24
New boots. Go on 1.

27
Travel all night. Go on 2.

28
Angels all around. Fly on 3.

29

30
Gift missing. Go back to 23 to find it.

END

31

Christmas poem

Can you guess the missing words?
The shape gives a clue.
Can you find the right sticker to fit each shape?

Let us travel to Christmas

By the light of a

Let us go to the hillside

Right where the  are

Let us see shining

Singing from heaven above

Let us see   cradling

Her newborn

with love

Decorate this tree

Look for coloured balls and tiny stockings. Put a bright star on the top.